THE
SHERWOOD
MYSTERIES
THE GHOST OF PUDDING HILL

J. P. Darcey

Printed in the United States of America

Library of Congress Control Number:	2023906001
ISBN: Softcover	979-8-88963-510-9
e-Book	979-8-88963-511-6

Republished by: PageTurner Press and Media LLC
Publication Date: 07/20/2023

To order copies of this book, contact:
PageTurner Press and Media
Phone: 1-888-447-9651
info@pageturner.us
www.pageturner.us

CONTENTS

To Sara Louise Darcey and John Elliot
May your love flourish forever.

CHAPTER ONE

The Young Farmers Club

"Hello Joan, I missed you this weekend," said Chrissy as she sat next to her friend on the school bus. "Did you do anything exciting at your aunts?"

"Oh come on, there is never anything exciting happens at my aunts," replied Joan. "Anything new happened round here?"

"Nope, just a boring weekend without you!"

Chrissy Danvers and Joan Parsons lived in a small village in Nottinghamshire. They had been close friends for many years and shared many an adventure together. They had a way of seeking out trouble or trouble had a way of finding them.

"Hey, don't forget it's the *Young Farmers* meeting in Lexington tomorrow night," said Joan. "We are supposed to be going on a field trip and so it won't be as boring as sitting in the village hall getting a lecture on how to avoid getting chased by a mad bull or something."

Both girls laughed at the thought of some of the unexciting lectures the *Young Farmers Club* gave but they enjoyed the field trips.

Their families had persuaded them to go to the *Young Farmers Club.* Both their fathers were local farmers and both families came from a long tradition of farmers.

"How are you getting to the meeting, Joan?" asked Chrissy.

"That Pudding Hill on the way up to Lexington is a terrible hill to try and ride your bike up."

"My mum is driving me. I'm sure she won't mind giving you a ride there and back as well."

"Thanks, my dad is busy tomorrow night so he wouldn't have been able to take me."

Chrissy's parents were divorced. Chrissy lived with her father and two older sisters, Elizabeth and Susan, although Susan was presently away at college.

"Hey Joan, we will be coming home tomorrow from Lexington in the dark. Maybe we might see the *Ghost of Pudding Hill.*"

"Oh you and your ghosts, that's only a legend."

"I've heard about people who have said they have seen it."

"Yea, maybe those people had one pint of beer too many or something when they saw it," laughed Joan.

"Well I'm going to look out for it tomorrow night," Chrissy snapped.

"Okay, if that's what you want."

Tuesday evening arrived. The girls enjoyed the field trip with the *Young Farmers Club.* Chrissy had found it particularly interesting because the trip was round Ponsomby Hall farm, the home of Col. and Mrs. Andrew Hawthorne. Col. Hawthorne loved to tell people about the interesting history of Ponsomby Hall and the farm. It was a very old house and quite a number of Lords and Ladies had stayed at the hall over the years. The grounds were known for the well stocked lakes and the herds of deer. The deer were now a protected herd and so there wasn't any hunting parties anymore but the Colonel did accommodate fishing clubs who fished the large lake for trout. Mrs. Katrina Hawthorne was well known for her lavish entertaining and the fishing clubs that usually had well to do members would gladly stay at the hall and pay for the luxurious accommodation and good food.

It was 9pm and dusk when Mrs. Parsons arrived to pick up the girls from the hall and of course Mrs. Parsons had to have one of her usual lengthy chats and a cup of tea with Mrs. Hawthorne. So by the time the three of them got on the road for home it was quite dark.

Of course Chrissy would not mentioned anything about looking out for the Pudding Hill ghost while Mrs. Parsons was in the car but she kept her eyes wide open and her senses were alert as they started the long windy descent down the hill.

About two thirds of the way down the hill, when Chrissy had started to give up hope of seeing anything she spotted a faint light going through the trees. It was

3

moving quite fast as though someone was riding with the light. She was quite frightened by what seemed to be an apparition but at the same time she was excited. She was positive it must be the Pudding Hill ghost.

The Pudding Hill ghost was supposedly a headless horseman. He had been beheaded by the king of his time for being a highwayman. As the legend said his spirit was known to ride his faithful horse up the hill on dark nights on an endless quest to seek revenge on the men who had caught him and turned him in to the king. The men were said to be from Lord and Lady Wakefield's estate, Egmund Hall, which was situated down a long lane some distance from the road to Lexington.

Egmund Hall still belonged to the Wakefields, Lord Matthew and Lady Carol Wakefield, were the current occupants.

Chrissy couldn't wait to get out of the car when they reached Joan's farm in Kirkby village where they lived. She whispered to Joan to ask her mother if she could walk part the way home with her so she could tell her what she had seen.

"Joan, I am sure I saw the ghost. We were about two thirds of the way down the hill when I saw a faint light going through trees like it was being carried by someone on horseback."

"You are letting your imagination get carried away with itself again, Chrissy."

"No I am not. I swear I saw something. We must

find out somehow, we must investigate."

"Here we go again, we must investigate."

"But look what good we did last time, Joan, when we found the Langford treasure for them."

"Well what do you suggest we do?"

"You know there is a hall at the top of Pudding hill, it's called Egmund Hall and it is owned by Lord and Lady Wakefield. Well there family has owned the hall for hundreds of years. I heard tell that the ghost had some association with the hall, in some way. Let's see if we can find out more about the legend," pleaded Chrissy.

"If it will keep you quiet we will go to the library in Ogmanton and see what we can find out about the legend and the Wakefield family. Ogmanton library has a section dedicated to local history, I'm sure we would be able to find out something there."

"Oh thanks, Joan. You're a pal and you know you can't resist an adventure, just like me.

Ogmanton was about three miles away from where the girls lived and was the place they attended school. It was the largest town in the area, the small villages like Kirkby and Lexington didn't have libraries or schools for senior pupils. Although Lexington had its own infant and junior school, Kirkby was even too small to have any school. The infants and juniors would go to school in Broughton, the village next to Ogmanton.

"So can we go on Saturday," asked Chrissy. "I am sure we can ride our bikes to Ogmanton."

"I'll find out from my mum to make sure we aren't doing anything. It should be alright. Anyway, I better get back my mum will be wondering where I have got to."

"See you tomorrow," shouted Chrissy as Joan disappeared down the street.

Won't this be exciting if we can find out anything about the Pudding Hill ghost, thought Chrissy. I hadn't heard from anyone recently that they had seen the ghost and so I wander why it is suddenly reappearing.

Chrissy skipped across the road to her house and proceeded round to the back of the house where the back door and outside sheds were. She was really looking forward to Saturday.

CHAPTER TWO

The Library

Saturday couldn't come quick enough for Chrissy. Life had been a bit boring since she and Joan had discovered the mystery behind the *shadow in the bell tower* and the Langford treasure. She was ready for more excitement. Maybe they could help another family in the neighbourhood like they had helped the Langfords. It was a very rewarding feeling to Chrissy being able to help people and it was even more rewarding having a mystery to solve in order to help the people concerned.

Chrissy and Joan arrived at the library in Ogmanton about 10 o'clock in the morning on the Saturday. They signed themselves in at the front counter and went straight to the local history section of the library.

"Okay Chrissy, you start in the E section and I will look in the W section," instructed Joan. "You are looking for anything on Egmund Hall and I will look for anything on the Wakefield family. It was the Wakefield family who built the hall about four or five hundred years ago I believe."

"Oh I do hope we find something," said Chrissy as she searched the E section.

It didn't take long for the girls to find books on the Wakefield family and Egmund Hall. They took the books to the study area of the library and proceeded to go through them to see if there was any mention of the Pudding Hill ghost.

"I can't find anything in this book," announced Chrissy, after spending about half an hour searching through a large book. "There is a lot of interesting history relating to the Egmund Hall but nothing about what we are looking for."

"No I can't find anything either. It appears that the Wakefields were well in with the monarchy throughout most of their history. Maybe we should sign these books out. Will you read up on Egmund Hall and I'll read up on the family."

"That sounds like a good idea, Joan but we must try and find out something about the Pudding Hill ghost, don't you agree?"

"Maybe there is a book on local legends and ghost stories or something. Let's look through the book shelves again? We may be able to piece something together by reading these two books and a book on local legends and folk lore as it would be called."

"You know I said that there wasn't any mention about seeing the ghost for a number of years and then suddenly I see something last night," announced Chrissy.

"There has got to be something behind him being seen again."

"I agree with you there, if you actually did see the ghost, you know your imagination Chrissy."

"I did see something, honest I did. Anyway, let's look through the books again!"

The two girls carefully went down the rows of books on local history to see what else they could find when suddenly Chrissy came across a book that might help them. It appeared to be quite an old book and it was called *Local Legends & Folklore.*

"I think I might have something," whispered Chrissy, remembering they were in the library and were supposed to be quiet.

"Let's have a quick look and if it looks any good, we will also sign this one out. I think we are allowed to sign out at least two books each."

"I don't have a library card yet," said Chrissy.

"You should have no problem getting one because you go to the local school and you have lived here a number of years. You just give them your name and address and what class you are in at school."

"Okay, come on and let's have a look if there is anything in this book."

Again, the girls took the books to the study area and quickly went through the pages. It would soon be lunch time and Joan nearly always had to be home on time for her lunch.

"Here we are," announced Joan. "*The legend of the Pudding Hill Ghost.* It also tells you how the hill got named *Pudding Hill.* Apparently there used to be an old lady who lived at the bottom of the hill about two hundred and fifty years ago. You know there is an old quarry at the bottom of the hill! Well, the old ladies husband was the night watchman at the quarry. She was known for sending him to work with puddings instead of bread and cheese."

"Funny old thing," laughed Chrissy. "He must have really liked his puddings."

"I think they eventually named the quarry *Pudding Hill Quarry.* A lot of places round here were built from stone from that quarry, so my dad said. He remembered when it was still open. Apparently, there are some of the old storage buildings still standing on the quarry site and I think Mister Pudding's work shed.

Joan and Chrissy laughed at Joan's nickname of the night watchman and then suddenly realised they better be quiet before they got thrown out of the library, without their books.

They collected up their three books and went to the librarian. Chrissy applied for a library card and both girls signed the books out for a week. They had to leave themselves time to read the books as well as get their homework done at night.

On the way home Chrissy asked Joan if she would mind if she read the book on *Local Legends & Folklore* as well as the one on Egmund Hall.

"Besides the book you have to read on the Wakefield family is much bigger and will take longer," stated Chrissy.

"That's true."

When the girls reached Joan's home, they agreed that they would stay at home that afternoon and start on the books. Besides it looked like rain and so they really couldn't do anything outside.

"I'll see you sometime tomorrow afternoon," said Joan. "We can catch up on what we've both read this afternoon."

"Sounds like a good plan, Smudge always likes to cuddle up with me on my bed when it's a rainy afternoon. He will be happy to have me at home."

Smudge was Chrissy's pet cat. The two of them were very close. Chrissy's mother had given her Smudge about a year past and that made Smudge even more special.

CHAPTER THREE

The Robberies

"Hello, their young lady," said Chrissy's father, Sam Danvers.

Sam was sat at the kitchen table having lunch with his other daughter, Elizabeth.

"You're a bit late miss," said Elizabeth. "We are supposed to have lunch together when we can. It's good for family relationships."

Oh we are getting proper, thought Chrissy about her sister who had just started to study for her exams to get top designations on certain subjects in school. But she didn't want to get into an argument and so she apologised, washed her hands and sat down for lunch. Smudge rubbed round her legs under the table.

"So, what have you been up too," asked Elizabeth. "Have you and Joan been getting up to more mischief?"

"No, we haven't and we don't get up to mischief."

Elizabeth and her father had a little laugh but dropped the subject of mischief as they knew it was a sore point with Chrissy.

"Joan and I have been to the library in Ogmanton, if you must know," announced Chrissy. "We are doing a project on Egmund Hall."

"Oh no, not another project," laughed Sam. "Maybe you might find some more treasure but just give me plenty of warning this time, remember I nearly got stabbed when I got involved in your LAST project."

"Dad don't remind me. That situation was awful. I was so scared."

Chrissy remembered the time they first discovered the Langford treasure and her father nearly got stabbed by Peter Cropston, who was actually a good friend to them now and often came down to help her father on the farm.

"Oh Dad," interrupted Elizabeth. "I was talking to Mrs. Baxter this morning she said that there have been some robberies in the district. Mrs. Cellars who lives in that big house in Lexington village was robbed, they took a lot of her good silver and some of the original artist paintings she had and jewellery. Also Mrs. Meadows up just outside Egmund village. They stole valuables from her as well."

"Oh, dear me," said Sam. "That's all we need in the district, a bunch of robberies. It's a good job we don't have anything of real value, except a few bits from your grand-parents on your mother's side but I don't think too many people know about them."

"I must make sure all the farm equipment is taxed and insured," continued Sam. "We are probably going to have police coming round and talking to everyone. You know how I forget about taxes and insurance, it was your mother who used to take care of all that stuff."

"I'll try and help you remember those things, Dad," interrupted Chrissy. "Susan is away at college and Elizabeth is busy with her exams. I will keep a calendar for you. I like organizing things."

"You never used too," laughed Elizabeth. "But it's all part of growing up and it's a nice thought, Chrissy."

Chrissy's family all knew that the last adventure Chrissy was involved in taught her some useful lessons about life. Lessons she had badly needed. They were all proud of her for that.

"Thank you, my dear daughter," said Sam. "Organizing dates for renewals and other things will be very helpful to me."

"Has anyone else been robbed, Elizabeth," asked Sam.

"Not that I know of but usually when there are a couple of robberies there is more to follow."

"Well, I think we should all watch out for anything suspicious. Make sure you mention it to Joan, Chrissy."

"Yes Dad. She has probably heard about the robberies as well."

CHAPTER FOUR

The Story of Egmund Hall & The Ghost

Chrissy managed to read through quite a lot of the book on Egmund Hall. It had been built by the Wakefield's about four hundred years ago and remained in the Wakefield family to this day. The Wakefield's were a noble family and known to the monarchy and dukes and duchesses throughout the ages. The hall was a large place and at one time had many a royal or noble visitor come to stay and take advantage of the shooting and the well stocked lakes. The grounds of Egmund Hall housed its own lake as did most noble houses of that era. She had heard that the gardens and grounds today were still well kept and a beautiful sight to see. She had never seen them herself.

Of course, the stories in the book of *Local Legends and Folklore* fascinated Chrissy the most. One of the stories mentioned the *Ghost of Pudding Hill* and that he was thought to have been the ghost of a highwayman called Dick Skeffington or Black Dick as he was known to some.

Dick Skeffington had lived about two hundred and fifty years ago and had been turned in to the king's men by a local noble family. He was sentenced to death for his wrong doings by the king's high court and for some reason the king had Black Dick beheaded instead of hung. His head had been displayed outside the city of Nottingham as an example to other highwaymen.

The story read that shortly after Black Dick's beheading a headless man riding a white horse was seen regularly riding up through the forest on Pudding Hill, he was never seen riding down the hill, just up. Legend said the apparition carried his head under his left arm and swung a lamp he held in his right hand back and forth.

Dick Skeffington had been a well-known highwayman in the district. He was well liked by the common folk as he would only steal from the wealthy and was quite often seen giving a poor family a basket of food and always spent his money in the local ale houses. All the common folk watched out for Dick and would warn him if the sheriff's or the king's men were seen nearby. Local folk thought the apparition was Black Dick because his true love lived somewhere nearby but it didn't say where or who his true love was. They believed he had come to find her and take her away with him. Dick had been a handsome man and many a fair maid had tried to win his love.

That was all that was said about the *Ghost of Pudding Hill* and so Chrissy hoped that Joan had found out more in the book about the Wakefield family. She was sure there must have been some connection.

Sunday afternoon Joan arrived at Chrissy's house at about two o'clock. Chrissy couldn't wait to question Joan about her research on the Wakefield's.

"So did you find out anything interesting in the book about the Wakefields."

"As we discovered before," replied Joan. "They were a well- known family to royalty and nobility but there was one particular story that interested me, it was about Sara Wakefield. She was the daughter of the Lord Wakefield about two hundred & fifty years ago. Apparently, she fell in love with a notorious highwayman."

"His name wasn't Dick Skeffington by any chance, was it?"

"Just a minute," said Joan, as she opened the book on the Wakefields at one of the pages where she had put a piece of paper as a marker.

Joan skimmed over the pages of the particular chapter in question.

"My goodness, his name was Dick Skeffington. Why do you ask?"

"Dick Skeffington was a notorious highwayman and had been captured by the king's men about two hundred & fifty years ago. He had been betrayed by a local nobleman that in turn led to his capture," Chrissy excitedly announced. "The King made no hesitation in having Dick tried for his crimes and sentenced him to death. He was beheaded."

Chrissy continued to tell Joan about what she had read in the book *Local Legends and Folklore.*

"Soon after Dick's beheading a headless horseman was seen riding up through pudding hill. He carried a lantern in one hand and held onto the horse's reigns with the other and under that arm he held his head."

"This all seems to fit together."

"Yes!" replied Chrissy. "The legend said that Dick was in love with a maid who lived in the area, and they believed that he was still going to see her after his death."

"His love must have been Sara Wakefield. It makes sense. After all her family would never approve of her being in love with a highwayman, it must have been Lord Wakefield who turned Dick Skeffington into the king's men. He must have had enough power to insist that he be put to death and that would end the relationship between his daughter and Dick."

"No wonder he died a restless spirit." Chrissy deduced. "That does explain the apparition I saw the other night when we were coming home from Lexington."

"But why would he suddenly be seen again, after all these years." Asked Joan "I wonder if it was the anniversary of his death or something. Do you think the Wakefields would talk to us about their history, or do you think they may be a bit ashamed about their ancestor, Sara being in love with a notorious highwayman?"

"How about we make an appointment to see them and use one of our phoney school projects again." Chrissy laughed but was quite serious.

"It's worth a try," said Joan. "Do you think your dad would let us use your telephone tomorrow after school? You are right, we should see if we can make an appointment to see Lord and Lady Wakefield. I have heard they are very nice people and not at all snobbish, but they are nobility."

"I'll ask Dad. I'm sure he won't mind."

"Anyway, Chrissy I best be off, we have relatives coming for tea and I have to get changed and be on my best behaviour."

Joan rolled her eyes back. She hated having to be so proper in front of some of her relatives.

"See you on the school bus tomorrow," Chrissy shouted after Joan as she headed out the back door.

"Yes, see you tomorrow."

CHAPTER FIVE

A Change of Plan

On the way home from school on the Monday, Chrissy remembered the story her father and sister had told her about the robberies that had been taking place locally.

"Did you hear anything about the robberies, Joan," Chrissy asked. "It's dreadful because whoever is doing it is picking on local wealthy ladies who live alone."

"Yes, my dad did mention something about it at teatime. I hope it's not going to happen to a lot of people because it must be awfully scary for ladies who are living by themselves."

"The local police officer Sergeant Doherty must be at sixes and sevens. He probably hasn't had so much going on in ages and he gets in such a flap sometimes."

The bus pulled up between Chrissy and Joan's houses, they lived at local farms just down the road from each other. Joan's house was a much larger house than Chrissy's. Joan's parents weren't short of extra money.

"Did your dad say it was alright to use the telephone to phone Lord and Lady Wakefield?" Joan Asked.

"Yes, he said it was okay, but he did give me a funny look. I think he decided not to question me about it though because he was in a hurry, and I am sure he thought he might be in for a big complicated story from me."

The girls laughed.

"I'll come over right now then, before I go home for tea."

The girls located the telephone number quiet easily in the local telephone directory. Chrissy picked up the phone and put on her best voice as she spoke to the operator.

"Hello operator! I wonder if you would put me through to Lexington 0543, please."

"One moment Miss, I will try and connect you to that number now," said the telephone operator.

Telephones were a luxury item for a lot of people at the time and so customers had to go through a telephone operator at the exchange.

Chrissy got connected to Lord and Lady Wakefield's housekeeper and so Chrissy explained briefly that she wondered if she could talk to Lord Matthew or Lady Carole Wakefield as she was doing a special project in history for school.

"One moment please, young lady," replied Rosaleena the housekeeper. "I go and talk to her ladyship."

Rosaleena was Italian. The Wakefields travelled a great deal and came across the wonderful efficient Rosaleena on their travels.

Chrissy waited patiently on the telephone. She told Joan that the housekeeper had gone to find Lady Wakefield. They crossed their fingers hoping that Lady Wakefield would give them an interview.

"Hello, young lady."

The voice at the other end of the phone was Rosaleena again.

"Her ladyship is so busy right now but she say you may leave your name and she will see you Wednesday evening about six o'clock, if you wish."

"Thank you! Six o'clock Wednesday evening will be most convenient," replied Chrissy in her over exaggerated posh voice. "My name is Christine Danvers and my friend who is working on the project with me is Joan Parsons. We go to the local Comprehensive School, and we live in the village of Kirkby."

"Do you know how to find Egmund Hall?" Rosaleena asked.

"Yes we do, we will ride up on our bicycles. The exercise is very good for us."

Chrissy said her goodbyes and put the telephone down.

"Oh yes miss posh boots," Joan laughed. "The exercise is very good for us."

The girls laughed at Chrissy's exaggerated politeness. It was a rare thing coming from Chrissy.

"Right, that's settled then, we will tell our parents we have an interview with Lady Wakefield regarding our history project. I do hope she will tell us something about Sara Wakefield and Dick Skeffington. Anyway, I must be off for tea and homework. I will see you tomorrow."

Chrissy walked out the door with Joan and waved her goodbye.

"Yes, I do hope Lady Carole Wakefield will be obliging," Chrissy said to herself in her posh voice. "I think I would make an excellent Lady Christine Danvers."

Smudge the cat appeared at the door when Chrissy walked into the kitchen. She looked at her mistress as if she was thinking, who do you think you are, using that posh voice.

Wednesday evening seemed to be a long time coming and Chrissy was glad that they were finally cycling down the long lane to Egmund Hall. When the hall came into view they stopped to look at the large building some distance in front of them.

The hall must have had about twenty bedrooms as well as stables and numerous outside buildings. Beautifully kept gardens and lawns reached down to a small lake by the way of a gravelled walkway and steps with statues each side of them. In the middle of the lake was a very ornate fountain of a boy holding a fish that had water coming out of its mouth.

"What a beautiful place," said Chrissy in amazement. "Could you ever imagine living there?"

"Yes, I could," Joan replied. "And you would fit in well with your posh voice."

Chrissy gave Joan a push and laughed.

"I thought my posh voice was excellent."

"Come on, it's a quarter to six. We better not be late; it would be very impolite."

The girls thought they better go to the back entrance of the hall. They didn't feel right leaving their bicycles at the bottom of the steps that led to the grand front entrance.

A large ornate cast iron bell was attached to the side of the back door. Joan pulled on the bell pull twice. It was so loud it seemed to echo through the inner courtyard of the estate. The door was opened by a large lady in a white apron.

"Yes, how can I help you," said the lady. "And before you ask, we are not buying anything or donating anything to any Charities at the moment."

"We are not selling anything or asking for any donations," said Chrissy indignantly. "We have an appointment to see Lady Carole Wakefield, but we didn't like to go to the front door with our bikes."

"Quite right as well," said the large lady. "That wouldn't do at all. I am Mrs. Midgely the cook by the way. And who are you two."

"I'm Joan Parsons and this is Chrissy Danvers. Lady Wakefield is expecting us."

"Leave your bicycles propped up against that wall and come into the kitchen. I will call Rosaleena to take you to Lady Wakefield. After all she is supposed to be the housekeeper, even though she is not English."

Mrs. Midgely sounded quite put out that an Italian lady was the housekeeper of this very old, very grand English house.

Chrissy and Joan stood by the large fire to warm their hands. The evening air was quite cool although it was invigorating.

It was quite some time before Mrs. Midgely reappeared in the kitchen and she seemed to be in quite an agitated state.

"Oh my, oh my," she bustled. "I'm afraid her Ladyship cannot keep her appointment with you today. She is in a dreadful state. I don't know why I hadn't heard sooner than this but apparently the house was burgled last night. His Lordship and her Ladyship are talking to Sergeant Doherty as we speak. There seems to be quite a number of valuable items missing. Oh dear, oh dear. Is no one safe in their beds anymore?"

The girls felt sorry for Mrs. Midgely, she was in a terrible state.

"We are so sorry to hear this, Mrs. Midgely," said Chrissy. "Would you like to sit down a moment? Maybe we can make you a cup of tea or something."

"That's very kind of you young lady but I must make some hot tea for them upstairs. Her Ladyship is near to tears, they stole some of her best jewellery which was not only precious but had a lot of sentimental value. Oh dear! Oh dear!"

"We'll help you make the tea," interrupted Joan. "You just sit and calm yourself for a while."

Mrs. Midgely took Joan's advice and told the girls where they could find everything.

After the tea was made and ready on a silver tray Chrissy and Joan said goodbye and informed Mrs. Midgely, they would contact her Ladyship another time.

"You are so understanding," cried Mrs. Midgely who was trying to stop the tears from flowing down her cheeks. "Thank you so much for your help girls. It was most appreciated and when you come again under better circumstances, I will make you tea and scones. Good-bye and thank you again."

When Chrissy and Joan were back on their bicycles and on their way down the long lane back to the road, they looked at each other puzzled.

"It seems like the local robbers are now robbing all rich people's houses. They are getting really bold," said Chrissy. "You know, Joan. I think we should start looking into this situation ourselves. Who knows, we might be able to help."

"Oh Chrissy, here we go again. But I do have to agree with you, it's a dreadful situation. You know what, you don't think the sudden appearance of the *Ghost of Pudding Hill* has anything to do with this. Do you?"

"It makes you wonder, doesn't it? It seems like an awful coincidence. Come on, let's go to my place, this calls for an emergency meeting."

CHAPTER SIX

The Interview

The following Monday Chrissy had an unexpected visitor. It was a young gentleman.

"Chrissy," Elizabeth shouted from the bottom of the stairs.

"There is a young man here to see you, he says he is from Egmund Hall."

Chrissy dashed down the stairs, nearly tripping over Smudge on the way down, and all the time thinking what young man would be visiting her from the Hall.

"Hello," said the handsome young man. "I am John Midgley, the cook's son from Egmund Hall."

"Pleased to meet you," said an astonished Chrissy.

"He doesn't look like a cook's son to me," she thought, "Smart and nicely dressed."

"I have a message from Lady Wakefield," he continued. "My mother asked if I would deliver it as I was on my way down to Kirkby."

"Oh, my dear girls," Mrs. Midgely greeted them warmly. "I will call Rosaleena, she will take you to her ladyship. Then hopefully you will stay and have fresh made scones and a cup of tea."

"Thank you, Mrs. Midgley," said Joan. "We would love to."

"You are looking well," Chrissy announced. "A lot better than you did the last time we saw you. What an awful situation. Have the police got any leads on the robbers yet."

"No, my dear," replied the Cook as she went to the inner door to find the Housekeeper. "We have heard nothing."

"Rosaleena has just gone to tell her Ladyship you are here then she will take you up to see her," Mrs. Midgely announced on her return.

It was exactly six o'clock when the girls entered Lady Wakefield's private sitting room.

It was a cozy room with a green carpet on the floor festooned in red roses and white For-get-me-knots. The walls were a warm sage green covered in family photos and some large landscape pictures. The tall, narrow, leaded glass windows were adorned in rich, red velvet curtains. In one corner of the room was an ornate but small writing desk and round the fireplace stood a long white, floral sofa and two armchairs in the same material. In front of the fireplace was a rich wood, oval coffee table, with two matching side tables at each end of the sofa.

"Do sit down," beckoned Lady Wakefield, pointing to the sofa. "I will see what I can do to help you with your school project."

"Thank you, your Ladyship," said Joan, as she and Chrissy entered the cozy room.

"Would you like some refreshment," asked her ladyship.

"No, thank you," replied Chrissy. "We will not keep you longer than necessary, we are sure you are a very busy lady."

Her ladyship nodded and they continued the interview.

The girls asked about who built the Hall and how long ago. Although they knew the answers, they had to make the project seem authentic.

Lord Wakefield was the Seventh Lord of Egmund Hall. The sixth Lord had been a bit of a scoundrel and gambler, he had let the Estate get into a state of disrepair. The deer herd had started to die off and with out proper care they become sick. Plus, poachers had been stealing fish from the trout lake. The lake was down to only a few fish.

"When my husband inherited from his father, we had quite a lot of work to do. Luckily his father hadn't squandered all the money, and some had been left in trust for my husband."

"So, as you see we have nearly got everything back to its original condition," said Lady Wakefield. "The deer herd is replenished and healthy and the trout lake has been cleaned and restocked. And we have a new estate manager. John Midgely, he is very good."

"Yes, I have met him, your Ladyship." Said Chrissy. "He seems like a very nice man."

"Absolutely." Said Lady Wakefield. Her mood changed to sadness, and you could see a tear in her eye. "And now we have been robbed and some of our valuable taken."

"I know," said Chrissy and Joan.

"It's a terrible state of affairs and more robberies are happening," said Chrissy in a somber voice. "But we would like to know about the rumour of Dick Skeffington, the highway man being associated somehow with the Hall. Do you know anything about that your Ladyship."

"Yes," interrupted Joan. "We like to put in the bad as well as the good if you don't mind, your Ladyship.

"Ah, yes," Lady Wakefield had now composed herself. "I will tell you what I know."

About two hundred & fifty years ago, practically to the date, the present Lord at the time had discovered his daughter had been secretly meeting Dick Skeffington and they had fallen in love. His Lord and Ladyship were terribly shocked and worried about their daughter's reputation and their own. So, they locked her in her room.

Sara's room faced the top of the hill and the forest and Dick had taken upon himself to come to the house when it was dark and climbed up the ivy to see Sara. He did this several times but the Butler at the time had seen Dick do this and reported it to his Lordship. DICK got caught one night before he got to the Hall. Sara had seen this happening.

She heard that Dick had been handed in to the Kings men and by request of her father when he was found guilty at his trial, he was to be beheaded. Out of sorrow and desperation Sara threw herself out of her bedroom window and landed on the stones below.

Her mother had heard her screams and quickly ran out to her and heard her last words.

"If I can't be with him in life," whispered Sara. "I will be with him in death."

She took her last breath, and Dick Skeffington was beheaded.

"What a sad story," said Chrissy mournfully.

"I know," replied her Ladyship. "But you cannot have a titled lady running away with a highway man. The same applies in these times. It's shame to the family."

Chrissy and Joan just lifted their eyebrows and looked a bit astonished, but they didn't say anything. When a knock was heard on the sitting room door.

"Come in," said Lady Wakefield.

hill, still looking for Dick."

"Did you know that Dick's ghost has been seen riding through the woods and up the hill again," said Chrissy. "I wonder why."

"I wonder if its an anniversary or something," Joan implied.

They all looked at each other and shook their heads.

It was now getting quite late, so they said their farewells to Mrs. Midgely and went on their way.

The girls were so excited and chatted about what had transpired, all the way home.

CHAPTER SEVEN

On the Look Out

Crissy didn't sleep well that night, she kept thinking about the robberies and how far would these men go before they stop. People were becoming quite frightened because these men would come into their homes even if they were in bed asleep. She feared that someone could get hurt.

She decided that night she would go on a secret lookout at some one's house, some one who would be a likely victim.

When Chrissy got on the school bus that morning, she decided she would tell Joan her plans but no one else.

"I heard there was a big Women's Institute anniversary do in Egmund Village Hall this evening," said Joan. "Mrs. Bexley had been the Egmund Village President of the Chapter for Fifty years and she was going to get an award for her services."

Chrissy quizzically looked at Joan and wondered what she was, to do with a look out. Then she realized that Mrs. Bexley lived just outside of Egmund and she had a nice big house and a bit of land. She rented the land to local farmers after her husband died but she still had the outbuildings. What a fantastic place to hide out with a good view of the house.

So, she told Joan that is where she would go tonight. Her father was out with the local darts club and her sister was visiting a friend in Ogmanton.

"I'll go up just before dark, so I can see where I am going without causing to much disturbance," she whispered to Joan. "I am going to go the other way, not up Pudding Hill. Then I can get settled in the barn opposite the house. The front door is on the side of the house as well. You can see it from the barn."

"You don't know if she has a house alarm do you," she asked Joan.

"Not that I know of. Although people are starting to get them."

"Even if she does have an alarm, I think the robbers will still have a go at her house," said Chrissy. "I heard that they even disarmed Mrs. Hennell's at Lexington. These men are ruthless."

Joan told her she must be very careful, just as the bus pulled in at the front of the school.

That evening, after Sam Danvers and Elizabeth left the house, Chrissy prepared herself a flask of hot soup and a sandwich and, put them in her backpack. She was preparing herself for a long evening and it could get cold even though it was late spring. She also put a flashlight and another coat in the backpack and set off on the road at the other end of the village, up to Egmund.

She arrived at Mrs. Bexley's just as it was getting dark and hid her bike in the hedge near Mrs. Bexley's house. The barn was right in front of the front door, she could also see the kitchen door at the other end of the house.

"This will be a great location," Chrissy whispered to herself, as she settled at the side of the upper door in the barn loft. The door was where the men would load bales of hay and other things for the winter storage.

Chrissy had been waiting for about an hour and nothing was happening.

"Mrs. Bexley will be home if they don't get here soon," whispered Chrissy. "Maybe they are not going to do this house."

Suddenly a black van with a roof rack on it, pulled into the yard. They had no lights on so they must have been up to no good.

She held her breath in anticipation.

"Hey Charlie," she heard someone say. "This one hasn't got an alarm yet."

"She will regret not getting one by the time we have finished," laughed Charlie.

They broke open the front door and went inside the house.

Chrissy quietly made her way down the barn steps and went to look at the back of the black van. She pulled a piece of paper and a pencil out of her pocket and wrote down their license plate number. She knew she couldn't

"Oh, there is my beautiful home," said Chrissy out loud. "Now hopefully Dad and Elizabeth are not back yet."

She made her way to the back door, everything seemed quiet as she let herself in the house and dashed upstairs to her bedroom. She collapsed on her bed and sighed a huge sigh of relief.

CHAPTER EIGHT

In a Bit of a Pickle

The next morning on the school bus Chrissy told Joan everything that had happened the night before. Her seeing the robbers and jumping on top of the van. Driving down Pudding Hill and the Ghost.

At this stage Joan's mouth was wide open in horror at the stories Chrissy was telling her.

"So, it appeared the headless horseman was staring straight at you," gasped Joan.

"I was horrified," said Chrissy. "I nearly wet my knickers."

Then she went on to tell Joan about Charlie driving into the old quarry, and them getting out at one of the old huts and going inside.

"That's when I took the opportunity to escape as quick as I could," gasped Chrissy. "I ran nearly all the way home, just stopping to catch my breath."

"You do some crazy things, Chrissy," Joan remarked. "It's a pity I can't go with you, but I would never be able to sneak out of the house. It's like Fort Knox at our

When they arrived at the location Chrissy had left the bike, she searched everywhere for it.

"Dad," Chrissy cried out. "I think someone has stolen my bike. I know I left it here."

"Let's go and see if Mrs. Bexley's in," said Sam. "She might know something about it."

Chrissy got a bit agitated at having to see Mrs. Bexley, because she knew she had been robbed but, she had to go along with her father to ask.

Sam knocked on her front door. Mrs. Bexley answered quite promptly but she was in quite a state.

"Mr. Danvers," she mumbled. "How can I help you. I am sorry I am in quite a state, I was robbed last night."

Sam looked at Chrissy quizzically. "Did you see anything, Chrissy."

"No dad," said Chrissy. She kept fidgeting and moving from one foot to the other.

"What's the matter with you girl," Sam asked his daughter. "You look a bit irritated, are you sure you didn't see anything."

"I am sure, dad." Said Chrissy. "It must have happened after I left my bike. I wonder if they might have stolen my bike as well."

"Calm down," she thought. "What would they want with her old bike."

She really hated these lies but what could she do. Her father would definitely stop them going to the quarry on Saturday afternoon.

"I am sorry to hear those awful men got to you as well." Sam asked Mrs. Bexley if they had taken much.

"They got some valuable painting," answered Mrs. Bexley, who was nearly in tears. "And they went up to my bedroom and took some of my good jewellery and, even found the money I had put under my mattress for emergencies in case I couldn't get to the bank."

"Oh, its really too much," she now wept.

"We are sorry to have bothered you at a time like this," said Sam. "Now you go inside and make yourself a cup of tea and if there is anything I can do, let me know. Have the Police been yet?"

"Yes," she whispered. "They came this afternoon. Oh, and I think they took a bike. Wondering if it had anything to do with the robbery. Oh, thank you for the offer of help Mr. Danvers."

She quietly closed the door, which had now been fixed after the break in.

Sam looked at Chrissy.

"Well, we will have to go down to the Police Station in Ogmanton," said Sam. "That's where your bike would have gone, as it is the nearest Station."

Chrissy had such a guilty look on her face, it made Sam wonder. But he left things as they were. They got in the van and went home.

"You know the Police will question you about this," explained Sam, as they walked into the kitchen at their house.

"Why dad," said Chrissy who wasn't thinking straight at all.

"Because your bike was at the scene, silly."

She nodded her head; she did feel silly and a bit stupid not thinking that the Police would find her bike.

"Sorry dad," she simply said, and went upstairs to her bedroom.

On the bus the next day she had to break the news to Joan about her bike.

"When is your dad going to take you to get it", enquired Joan.

"Hopefully tonight. It will ruin all our plans if I don't get it tonight. I do hate lying to my dad but if anything goes wrong, and we don't find anything at the quarry, the robbers might hear of our investigation and make a run for it."

"Yes," said Joan. "I agree with you there. I am sure they have a good stash of valuables that would make quite a few Pounds."

That afternoon when Chrissy got home from school, she approached Sam about going to the Police Station after tea.

"Joan and I wanted to go for bike ride," she said. "For a change Joan hasn't got to go anywhere Saturday afternoon."

After tea, just as they were about to leave for Ogmanton, a Police car pulled into the farmyard.

"Well, Christine," said Sam. "It looks like the Police have found out who the bike belongs to, by themselves. This does not look good. Just be careful what you say, or they are going to involve you in that robbery at Mrs. Binkley's."

Chrissy was shaking inside with nerves. It was bad enough having to lie to her father, but to the Police, the thought was terrifying.

"Miss. Christine Danvers," said the officer. "I am Constable Beamer.

His lifted Chrissy's bike out of the boot of the squad car.

"We believe this bike might belong to you."

Chrissy looked a bit puzzled, "how did he know the bike was mine," she thought.

"Sergeant Doherty recognized, it," said Constable Beamer. "He said he sees you and Joan Parsons riding around on your bikes a lot."

"Yes, that's mine," said Christine sheepishly. "I had to leave it on the top road, outside of Egmund, I had a flat tire and had to walk home."

The Officer checked the bike out and found no flat tire. Sam and Constable Beamer both glared at Christine.

"What are you talking about Christine," questioned Sam. "There is no flat tire on this bike."

"But Dad, the bike was wobbling all over the place. It was getting dark and so I didn't want to stand there messing about with it, so I pushed it in the hedge. You

"I dare not straighten it, Chrissy, in case you have twisted it badly."

"How am I supposed to get around, may I ask."

"Look, maybe I might find an old cart or something and I will pull you around."

Although it was a serious, situation they both couldn't help but laugh at the thought of Joan pulling Chrissy around on an old cart like they would have done when they were kids.

"Right Chrissy," said Joan. "I am going to help you stand up. But don't put any weight on your right foot."

"I think you're safe there, I don't think I could bear any weight on my right foot."

After a great deal of moaning and groaning and getting her balance. With Joan's help Chrissy managed to put her arm round Joan's neck and balance herself on her left leg.

They struggled over to a wooden crate where Chrissy could sit comfortably. Joan found a smaller crate for Chrissy to put her right foot on. Joan folded what remained of Chrissy's raincoat and put it on the smaller crate so Chrissy could comfortably rest her lower leg and foot.

"You're a proper nurse, aren't you," said Chrissy as she settled in a more comfortable position, even though she was in a lot of pain.

Joan blushed.

"Right," said Joan. "I am going to try and find something that we might be able to wheel you around in. I will also make sure the robber's van is not around. We don't want to run into them."

"I don't think they will be. When they found the money at Mrs. Binkley's they said they were going to have a few drinks today. To celebrate."

"Let's hope they are good and drunk by now then," said Joan.

Chrissy waved Joan off and sat quiet, while she contemplated how serious her injury was. It really hurt. She wished she had two Aspirin or something. She did have water though and so reached in backpack for one of the bottles of water and drank of it thirstily.

"It's a good job I didn't land on my back," thought Chrissy. "I would have broken the bottles of water and my torch."

Joan seemed to be taking ages, but it was a big site and a large area to go round. She returned about half an hour later pulling what looked like a converted old pram and a smile on her face.

"Right Chrissy," explained Joan. "We will lift you on this old pram. Look they took the hood off it. I will just raise it up a little bit, so you are not sat right in the bottom."

Joan put a few pieces of wood in the bottom of the pram and then carefully took Chrissy's raincoat from under her foot and put that on top.

Chrissy was wondering how she was going to sit in the pram, but Joan had that covered.

"Okay," she said. "I will lower the bottom of the pram and then we will move you round so you can sit in it. Then I will lift you."

Chrissy didn't say a word. She just followed Joan's instructions and was lowered down on the bed of the pram.

"Now hold on to the sides," said Joan. "And I am going to try to lift you up until the pram is on all four wheels."

Slowly Joan lifted the pram up to the four wheels and then pulled Chrissy nearer to the top of the pram, so she was balanced correctly. She then found another piece of wood that was flat and long enough to fit under Chrissy's leg. With some pieces of the lining of Chrissy's raincoat that she had left, she tied Chrissy's leg to the flat piece of wood and secured the wood to the pram.

"I am absolutely amazed, Joan Parsons," said Chrissy. "You have quite an inventive mind. Now, let's see if you can push me alright."

It worked! The ground was a bit rocky in places but, overall, it wasn't too bad. Years of heavy lorries driving over it had made it quite flat and firm.

They first looked through the window of the nightwatchman's hut, but it wasn't big enough to store anything much. Then they went on to the next long hut that was going towards the side of the quarry where there seemed to be a cave of some sorts.

The first long hut didn't appear to have anything in it but junk and bits of wood. Joan tried the door, but it wouldn't open so she checked through the few windows that were round the hut. They then went to the second hut. Again, it was just junk, pieces of wood and a few stones. It was the same at the next hut. Nothing!

Feeling quite disheartened they went on to the fourth hut in that row, but Joan hit a rock she had not seen, and the pram went over on its side, tipping Chrissy onto the ground.

"Oh, Chrissy," cried Joan. "I am so sorry I didn't see that rock."

The old pram was now in quite a state of disrepair. Joan helped Chrissy into the cave, that was next to the last hut in that row. They found a nice smooth rock for Chrissy to sit on comfortably, then Joan got a crate she could put Chrissy's leg and foot on.

"I am sorry," said Joan. "But we are getting nowhere fast and it's getting late. I am going to have to get help."

"You have to be careful who you tell," pleaded Chrissy. "Who can you tell without causing any alarm."

The two of them sat thoughtfully for a minute.

"What about your dad, Chrissy."

"Oh gosh he would probably disown me, but if you have to tell anyone I suppose it is better that it is him."

down the passageway, but she couldn't see an end to it. Gradually she managed to get about six feet down the passage, but she still couldn't see an end.

"I don't want to get lost," she thought. "I better not go any further."

She carefully made her way to her make do seat and footrest and lowered herself down.

"I am so hungry still," she whispered. "I will eat the other bag of crisps, then hopefully I will manage till Joan comes back. They say you can live without food for quite a long time, but not water."

After Chrissy had finished the crisps and drunk a bit more water, she sat quiet and contemplated everything that had been going on for the last week or so. She thought about the *Ghost of Pudding Hill.*

"Oh, I hope he doesn't come near the quarry," Chrissy cried out loud. "It is dark now and that is when he comes out. I would die if I saw him, and I can't run away. What would he do to me? I suppose scare me to death. Oh, *Heavens to Betsy.*"

Chrissy persuaded herself that she was just getting excited about nothing. Why would the ghost come through the old quarry yard.

"He probably gets down to the bottom of Pudding hill and disappears," she thought.

As she calmed herself down, she started to close her eyes again and doze off.

Chrissy sat in that state, in and out of sleep until a sound coming from the long passageway of the cave suddenly brought her round to full consciousness. She sat upright abruptly.

"What was that" she whispered.

Noise was coming down from what must be the back of the cave. It got louder and louder. Then she was able to identify the sound, at least she thought she could identify the sound.

"It sounds like a horse, with a heavy load on it's back," she thought. "It's the headless horseman, the ghost and his ghost horse."

She struggled and got out of her seat; she didn't know what she was going to do.

"Maybe I will press myself against this wall over here and he might not see me."

So, she pressed herself tightly against the wall, that would be the end of the short part of the L.

She froze and didn't move, hardly breathing. But as the sound got closer and closer, she got more and more frightened about what could happen.

"Would this be her last day on earth," she quietly cried. Tears running down her face. "I am sorry to have been such a nuisance dad. I only wanted to help people. Joan, please come back and frighten this deathly spirit away."

She held her hands together in prayer.

"Mum, I wish you were here, I miss you so much."

As the sound got closer and closer, she knew it was a horse. She felt something warm and wet run down her inner thighs. She had wet herself; she couldn't help it.

As the sound was coming closer and closer towards her, she could see coming round the bend in the cave a white horse with a headless man on top of it. He wore a black cloak and in one hand he held the reins and carried his distorted head under his arm. In the other hand he held a lantern which he shone straight at her.

"This is it," cried Chrissy.

Everything went black as she fainted in a heap on the hard cold earth.

The ghostly figure got down from his horse, put the lantern on the ground and his head where Chrissy had been sitting. He then took of his cloak and pulled his black tunic up over himself.

This was no ghost but an ordinary man. Quite well dressed as well, with medium brown corduroy trousers and a neatly ironed checked shirt. He bent down to Chrissy. She was out cold, and it looked like she had a bad injury to her ankle and foot.

He recognised who she was.

The man carefully lifted Chrissy on his horse and put her arms each side of the horse's neck so she wouldn't fall. He then picked up his lantern and climbed up behind her so he could hold her straight. He left his false head behind on the rock. It was hard enough holding the lantern and Chrissy, never mind a head.

He rode out of the cave towards the back of the quarry, and a wire fence that must have been the outskirts of the quarry. Without getting off the horse he removed a couple of clips that were holding the fence up. He pulled the fence back, just enough for them all to get through and then clipped the fence back in place again.

About three hundred yards in front of them was an old cottage. He pulled up in front of the cottage and dismounted the horse, then lifted Chrissy's limp body off his back. Wrapping the horse's reigns round a nearby pole while he struggled holding on to Chrissy, he opened the cottage door and walked in.

It was a sparsely furnished abode but there was a bed with some blankets on it in one room where he was able to lay Chrissy down comfortably.

He then returned to his horse and took her round to the back of the cottage where there was a sizeable shed scattered with straw. He took the horses saddle off and gently rubbed her down and then gave her some feed. Patting her on the back, he then returned to the cottage.

Chrissy was slowly coming round.

"I am on a comfortable bed," she whispered. "This looks like an old cottage but cosy. Where am I, how did I get here?"

Chrissy remembered seeing the ghost.

"Well, I don't think I am dead," she whispered again.

The man walked into the room just as Chrissy was coming to.

She immediately recognized him and although she was overwhelmed, she sighed a sigh of relief.

"John Midgely," she said in a surprised voice. "What are you doing here? Where am I?"

"Yes, Miss Christine Danvers, its I."

"Let me just check out your foot and get you something to eat," said John. "Then you get those wet things off and wrap a blanket round yourself. The soup will be in the kitchen ready for you and then I will tell you, my story."

He nodded down to her jeans, it seemed he didn't want to embarrass her.

John unwrapped the makeshift bandage on Chrissy's ankle and foot and revealed the true nature of her injury.

"Oh, my goodness," was all that Chrissy could say.

"This is a bad injury; you should really be going to hospital."

"Joan didn't tell me it was that bad, she just said that she thought the ankle might be twisted."

"She probably didn't want to frighten you." Said John. "I have some Dettol disinfectant. We will clean the area up with the disinfectant and water. I should have some clean bandages somewhere as well."

Once John has cleaned Chrissy's foot and put a dressing and tensor bandage on it, he went into the kitchen. John got some wood started a nice fire in the hearth. He then put a saucepan of soup on the old hob next to the fire.

Chrissy took off her wet jeans and knickers in the bedroom and wrapped a blanket tightly round her waist. She found an old tie in one of the dressers and secured the blanket with the tie. Being a bit cold she also wrapped a blanket round her shoulders. Walking into the kitchen she felt a warmth coming from the fire and a heavenly smell of chicken soup *her favourite.*

"Sit down here," beckoned John. "And I will tell you my story, then you can tell me why you were in the cave at the quarry."

He handed Chrissy a warm bowl of soup and some fresh crusty bread.

He told Chrissy that it was he, that was the *Ghost of Pudding Hill,* at least the current one. He was in love with Lord and Lady Wakefield's daughter, Sara. The current Sara that is.

They both knew that Lord and Lady Wakefield would not approve of their union, with him being the cook's son. So, they decided to meet secretly at the summer house at the Hall two or three times a week. We came up with the idea of me dressing as *The Ghost of Pudding Hill.* I had heard of the legend, passed down from generation to generation.

So, he continued. He bought himself a fine white horse, a friend of his, Sandy Smith, was selling. He gave her a good price for him. I called him Pegasus.

"The one in Greek mythology," interrupted Chrissy. She was riveted to her seat and supping the warm soup.

"Yes, that is the one."

He told her that he also had a friend who worked in the costume department of a Theatre in Nottingham, Phil. He got me the cloak and tunic, and the distorted head. The tunic had holes in it for your eyes, so you could see.

John continued to tell Chrissy, that since Sara and himself had fallen in love, he had inherited his uncle's quite substantial farm at the end of the village. His uncle had no heir and John being his sister's eldest, it was rightfully his. But Sara's father had said that there were no suitable eligible bachelors near where they lived, so he was sending her down to stay with her mother's sister in London.

Sara has tried to talk to her father about our situation and how it has improved immensely with my inheritance, and would he consider me as a suitable match for her. But he wouldn't listen to her.

"You see," John said sadly. "I am also the manager of Lord Wakefield's own estate, as well as my own small estate."

"Will you help us catch some robbers," asked Chrissy. "Then you will be hero as well. I am sure that would help. And Joan and I will speak up for you."

"Of course, I will," said John. "Are these the men that have been robbing local estates and rich widows."

"Yes!"

"Is that why you were hanging on the top of that van, the other night." Said John.

Chrissy told John about her doing a stake out at Mrs. Binkley's and that she had decided to jump on top of their van and hang onto the roof rack. She wanted to find out where they were going with the proceeds from their recent robbery. And she had seen the ghost, *yourself*, she added. And had been terrified then, as she was when he found her the cave.

"When is your friend coming back for you," asked John.

"I thought she would have been back ages ago, but something must have delayed her."

"She is going to be very shocked when she finds my distorted head, where you were sitting."

"Oh goodness, she will be horrified," replied Chrissy.

Although it was a frightening and serious business, they couldn't help but chuckle about it.

So, that is why you were in the cave and on top of that van," said John. "You are trying to find where the robbers had stashed their ill-gotten gains."

Chrissy continued to tell him about hiding her bike, and the police finding it. And having to tell lies to the Police and her father and how she hated telling lies, even small ones. She mentioned that if the Police found out where the robbers had gone after Mrs. Binkley's robbery and the robbers found out the Police knew, they would just load everything up that they had stolen and run.

"You see," said Chrissy. "I couldn't risk that anyone other than Joan knew where their stash was. I don't think they are local men and I think they must sell the stolen goods on to someone they know."

She told John that it was the quarry that they had come to, the night he had seen her hanging on top of the van. They had unlocked the gates at the roadside and then drove to one of the huts. They wanted to have a drink first to calm their nerves after seeing *The Ghost of Pudding Hill.*

They both laughed.

"That is when I got off the top of the van," Chrissy continued. "And ran nearly all the way home. I was terrified that I might see the ghost again and I needed to get away from those men."

She then mentioned about their plan to go to the quarry today and see if the stolen goods were in one of the yard huts. She told him how she had fallen of the Signalman's ladder, about four feet from the ground and that was how she injured her foot. She told him that Joan had found an old pram to wheel her around in, but it broke down after a while.

They both laughed again.

"We had searched the first row of huts but found nothing," she said. "But we still have to search the second row. It was then getting dusk and that is when Joan thought it better if she went to get help from my dad. You would like my dad; he is a lovely man."

"Okay Chrissy," said John. "I think the best plan of action right now is for me to go and see where your dad and Joan are. I have a bike here so I can cycle to Kirkby."

"John," cried Chrissy as she grabbed hold of his arm. "Don't go to Joan's house at this time of night. Her parents are not very understanding. Go straight to my house. If my dad has been out, he should be back by now. And don't let anyone else know what you are doing, please!"

John told Chrissy that she would be safe where she was because the cottage was his. It used to be his uncles first home until he went to Australia and had good fortune with farming.

It was decided what to do next. John put more wood on the fire and brought in more from outside. And that if she got tired to go and lay down on the bed but leave the door open so the heat would go into the bedroom. He told Chrissy that the toilet was outside, but he had a Porto-Potty in the back porch.

"Now lock the doors after I leave," said John. "And don't let anyone in apart from Joan, your father or me."

They said to each other, "See you soon." And John took off on his bike.

Chrissy felt very alone again, but she wasn't afraid. She knew who *The Pudding Hill Ghost,* was and she now felt very confident that they would find the robbers stash of stolen goods.

She got up and hobbled to the window in the kitchen and looked out. She couldn't see anything but when she opened the door, she heard voices. Familiar voices. It was Burt and Charlie; she would recognise those voices anywhere.

"They must have been out on their night drinking," Chrissy thought. "And now come back to check their loot."

She saw a light shining and heard their voices again.

"Here Charlie," said Burt. "Let's check on what we got and then we will just do that one more job tomorrow night, you know them at the big Hall, they had lots of good loot. And we hardly touched it the last time."

"That's taking a risk," said Charlie. "The same place twice. Mind you, Micky The Midget would be dead pleased with what we've got this time."

"Yea, and he better give us a good deal on it. Your good at numbers Charlie. You figure it out for us."

"Aye, a will Burt. When we've done the Hall tomorrow."

Chrissy knocked over a chair near the door. She was kneeling on it trying to hear what they were saying. It made a loud bang on the flagstone floor.

Charlie and Burt looked up and saw the light in the cottage. Chrissy could see them looking through the fence. Quickly she found a piece of paper and a pencil in a drawer by the window and wrote down.

*The Wakefield's Egmund Hall, tomorrow
night. Last Job. The loots in the second hut,
last row by the fence.*

She quickly grabbed her jeans, which were still a bit damp but what could she do, then she put the note in her knickers leaving a bit of paper sticking out so it could be seen. Hobbling into the bedroom she sat down on the bed and put her jeans on.

"I know," she thought. "I will pretend I am asleep. It might work, then it might not but I will try."

"It's just not my day today," whispered Chrissy. "If they catch me goodness knows what will happen."

She quietly closed the bedroom door and put the blankets tightly over her and lay there like a stone from the quarry.

Unfortunately, she had unlocked the front door because she thought it was her father and John.

"Hey, Burt," said Charlie. "There's a light on over there. In that old cottage. Do ya think someone might have heard us."

"Don't know mate, we better go an have a look. Look, it looks like that piece of fence has been moved."

Burt went to investigate the fence and found that he could easily lift it from the bottom, and they could crawl through. Quietly they made their way to the cottage.

"Hey, Charlie," whispered Burt. "The door is unlocked."

He quietly opened the door and went inside, with Charlie close behind him.

"There is no one in here," whispered Burt.

"Try that room over there," Charlie whispered. "It's probably a bedroom."

They went into the bedroom and saw Chrissy covered in blankets. Burt poked her in the side. Chrissy sat up abruptly.

"Who the hell are you," she shouted and acted really surprised. "And what do you want."

"Never mind who we are," said Charlie. "Who are you and what ya doing here,"

"This is my granny's cottage; she'll be back here soon. She will set her big dog on you if you don't get out. The dogs like a wolf and I am *Little Red Riding Hood.*"

She sarcastically laughed at them and showed no fear, although she was shaking inside.

"What we going to do, Charlie. She's a cheeky brat."

"Here Burt, get hold of her and wrap her in one of those blankets. We will tie her up and put her in the hut with our loot. Then we will see if granny and the big bad wolf come along."

They both laughed at Charlie's pathetic joke.

Chrissy fought and thumped Burt to let her go but he was quite strong. Then when he came to moving her right leg, she screamed out loud because of the pain.

"What's the matter with you brat," shouted Charlie.

Although Chrissy could stand a lot of pain and was strong willed, Burt had really hurt her foot and it started to bleed.

"What have you done there, girl," asked Burt in a softer voice.

"I have broken my foot and twisted my ankle."

Chrissy was now crying in pain.

"Hey, Charlie, why don't we give her shot of that Brandy, she won't feel much pain then."

"Okay! You are just a big softie, aren't you Bertie lad."

"My sister has kids," said Burt. "They like me, they do."

Charlie rolled his eyes back and laughed. "Carry her over your shoulder. That way her foot will be just dangling there, mate. And bring a couple of those blankets, we don't want her getting pneumonia as well."

They left the cottage and closed the door behind them.

"We don't want granny and the *wolf* to know that she is gone as soon as she gets to the door." Said Charlie.

With the blankets covering Chrissy up they made their way back through the fence then up to the door of the second hut.

"I had been right," thought Chrissy.

As they entered into a long hut, she could see rows and rows of pictures in beautiful frames. A chest that she assumed had jewelry in it and pieces of gleaming silver.

Candelabras, platters, tea sets. All sorts of things that were worth a lot of money.

"What dirty scoundrels," thought Chrissy.

There was even a family picture they had stolen because it was in a beautiful silver frame.

"I'll put her up there in that top corner," said Burt. "Where's the Brandy, mate. I will give her shot of that then gag her with some of that bandage. We don't want her screaming for help."

"What are you going to do with me," cried Chrissy.

"When we have done that last job tomorrow and loaded up the van," said Charlie. "We will leave you here until we have gotten far enough away, then we will phone the pigs and tell them where you are, and we will get them to bring a doctor or someone to look at your foot."

"Now ain't that nice of us little girl," Burt said. "Now you take a good swig of this brandy, and it will help you, so you don't feel the pain. Won't it Charlie"

Burt laughed.

"Don't get her to drunk and hurry up and get that gag over her mouth."

"We will bring you something to eat in the morning and I will see if I can get some pain tablets," said Burt. "Now you give me that bottle of brandy and let me get this gag on you, brat."

Chrissy bit his hand while he was trying to get the gag on her. Burt shouted out and slapped her across the face.

"Now you watch it, brat. Here Charlie get me some thing to tie her hands behind her back."

Charlie found some rough rope on the floor. They made sure she was tied up tightly.

"Come on mate," ordered Charlie. "Bring that bottle of brandy and let's get back to the pub and bed. Hey, that barmaid there is a bit of alright, ain't she."

"Hey, I wouldn't mind taking her to me bed."

They laughed as they walked out through the door, closed it and locked it behind them. Chrissy could hear the van drive off. She was alone again, in the dark and tied up. The brandy was making her feel lightheaded and sleepy.

She must have drifted in out of sleep for an hour or two she thought until she heard a noise outside of the hut. She listened intently to see if she could identify the voices.

"That's my dad," she thought.

She couldn't cry out because of the gag.

She understood the other voice to be John. Sitting there wondering what to do she realised that it would not be wise to do anything. If she wasn't in the hut in the morning, they would know she had been found and get out of the area with the stolen goods and not do the Wakefield's house again.

"If Dad and John find my note, they will surely get the police up there," she thought. "And if John was with them, he would also be a hero. Then we can talk to Lord

Wakefield and explain what a worthy person John is and tell them about his inheritance."

Chrissy listened again. They seemed to have taken ages at the cottage. Then she heard them coming towards the fence again.

"Thank goodness Chrissy was able to write that note," said John. "We will be able to catch them in the act now."

"But where have they taken my Christine," said Sam. "She must be in a right state with that injury to her foot and ankle."

"Don't worry, Sam. They won't harm her or else they will be arrested for assault as well, and that would be a long stretch."

"Yes, I know you are right."

Chrissy's father sounded really upset. She wanted to bang on the side the hut, but she knew it wasn't the right thing to do.

"To catch those villains in the act, was the right thing to do," thought Chrissy. "They have upset enough people."

It was then quiet outside again. They must have left already. She wished she knew what time it was and how long she had to wait for Charlie and Burt to come back.

"I must try and get more sleep if I can. And dream about being safely in my own bed tomorrow night."

CHAPTER TWELVE

Left with the Loot

Chrissy woke a second time that night, she was in more pain again. The affects of the brandy were wearing off.

"It looks like it's dawn," she thought.

She started to feel miserable, tears were coming down her cheeks and although she had the blanket round her, she felt cold. She thought about the stupid situations she gets herself into. Maybe she shouldn't be so bold and brave in future.

It was her nature to be curious and adventurous, and she didn't believe in injustice to other people. She knew that if she could help someone she would. Even at risk to herself. She knew Joan was like that as well. She wasn't quite as bold as Chrissy, but she would always try to do what she could.

"I wonder what happened to Joan," she thought. "I bet her dad kept her in and he wouldn't give her the time to explain either, not if he were mad at her for some reason."

She tried to move her legs a little bit so she wouldn't stiffen up, but it was hard to move her right leg. She couldn't even look at her leg because her hands were tightly tied behind her back.

"I think I will count the paintings, to pass the time away," she decided.

She was amazed at how many there were, and she couldn't see the ones behind them. These men had come to make a small fortune out of our little communities.

"I wonder who *Micky the Midget* is," thought Chrissy. "He is obviously the middleman."

At last, a vehicle pulled up outside. Chrissy hoped it was Charlie and Burt's van. The door to the hut opened and there they were.

"Here go and give her that sandwich for breakfast," said Charley. "And some water and a couple of those pills for pain."

"I will have to take that gag off, what if she cried out and granny and the *wolf,* are in."

"Go and check the cottage out then stupid. And don't be long we have to get this lot loaded up before we do the last job later."

"Yea, and I want a good dinner," said Burt. "Before we go and do the job and head straight of to Nottingham."

"You are always thinking of your stomach, Burt. Now go and get that cottage checked out."

Burt wasn't gone too long before he came back and informed Charley that all was clear. He then went over to Chrissy and took the gag off and let her bite on the sandwich.

"I am not untying her; she might try and escape."

"And how far do you think she is going to get with a broken foot, stupid," said Charlie laughing. "She is more likely to bite you. Remember her granny has got a wolf."

Burt quickly looked at Chrissy, Chrissy growled at him.

"Give me the sandwich," she said. "Or I will bite you."

After she had finished her sandwich, he gave her a couple of pain tablets and a good drink or water. He then gagged her again before he went to help Charlie load up the van.

"Hey Charlie. We are not going to get all this stuff in the van. What are we going to do."

"Did you look in the local paper to see if there were any trailers for sale, like I asked you." Charlie was getting really angry now.

Burt just shook his head.

"You would think I'd have found you under a gooseberry bush. You just don't think sometimes, mate."

They decided to load what they could in the large black van and then come back with a trailer that they could hook on the back of the van. They said they would bring Chrissy something more to eat.

Again, Chrissy was alone and waiting. The pain tablets had given her some relief, enough to let her rest again for a while. At least now the daylight sun had come in through the windows and warmed the hut up a bit.

A couple of hours later Charlie and Burt returned.

"Now go and give her something to eat," said Charlie. "And let's get on. It must be mid afternoon now. We must check with someone locally if there is anything going on at the Hall tonight. We will ask at the pub up the road, *The Horse & Plow* I think it's called. We can walk there and back, and you can have your big dinner."

"That sounds like a good plan," Charlie. "Eeeh you are smart mate. You always have everything sorted."

Charlie rolled his eyes back and shook his head.

Burt went to give Chrissy another sandwich and sausage roll.

"Another sandwich," said Chrissy. "I want a good dinner as well. Are you sure you can't take me to the pub as well. You could piggyback me, Burt. I promise I'll be good."

"Don't be stupid, girl," said Charlie. "You will get a good meal when they rescue you."

"Yeah, someone might see us, and wonder why I am giving you a piggyback," commented Burt. "What a stupid idea."

Charlie rolled his eyes back again, then got on with clearing the hut. After Burt had finished seeing to Chrissy, he gave her a couple more tablets then went to help Charlie.

The last few articles were put in the trailer and then they closed and locked the doors. They left room in the van for the items they planned on stealing from the Wakefield's.

Before they could leave again Chrissy shouted out in desperation. She mumbled through her gag that she needed to go to the toilet.

"What did you say girl."

"Take the gag off, man and let her talk."

"What did you say girl," asked Burt when he removed the gag.

"I want to go to the toilet," shouted Chrissy in Burt's ear.

"Take her round the back of the hut, you will have to untie her hands though. But put her gag back on."

"Come you," said Burt.

"You will have to carry me Burt, I can't walk, can I."

"I will be glad when we are rid of her," moaned Burt. "She is a dam nuisance."

Burt picked Chrissy up and put her over his shoulder and went round to the back of the hut. He untied her hands and leaned her against the fence.

"Now get on with it Brat, I feel like a ruddy babysitter and you're a big baby."

Burt turned his back, but Chrissy felt a bit

uncomfortable and couldn't pee. She tapped him on the shoulder and pointed for him to go further away. Luckily, he understood her muttering and moved.

"You were long enough," shouted Charlie when they returned to the hut.

"She couldn't go because I was standing to close," said Burt. "Let me put her back in the corner and let's go. She is driving me batty."

Chrissy wasn't amused but she had to laugh. She was really getting under Burt's skin.

He plonked her back in the corner and tied her hands behind her back again.

"Now shut up and stop being a pest."

Burt stomped out of the hut, slammed the door and locked it behind him.

An hour or two later Chrissy was dozing on and off again when she heard someone knocking at the window. She sat upright and felt quite alarmed, the window was just across from her.

It was Joan. How was she to tell Joan not to hang around. She thought Charlie and Burt were supposed to be back soon. She shook her head from side to side, then she kept moving it forward as if to push her away.

Chrissy heard noises coming from near the gate. She was hoping that Joan had also heard them. Again, she shook her head and moved her head forward to try and indicate to Joan, she wanted her to go away and hide.

Joan finally understood when she heard the voices

herself. She quickly made herself scarce. Just as Burt unlocked the door.

"Well, this is goodbye brat, I hope your foot gets better soon. Here I've brought you a Yorkshire Pudding with gravy on it."

"They will rescue you sometime tonight. When we are far away from here."

"Charlie said we will probably go to Spain for about a month while things quiet down. Who knows we might come back up here next year."

Burt laughed and took her gag off so she could eat the Yorkshire Pudding. Then he gave her two more pain tablets and water and gagged her again.

"See ya, brat. I suppose I better leave this door unlocked so they don't have to break it down to rescue ya."

He went outside laughing and as he shut the door behind him. Chrissy could hear the van start up and drive away. She sighed a sigh of relief.

A short time later Joan came running into the hut.

"Oh Chrissy, I am so sorry," she cried. "My dad was in a right mood last night and he wouldn't hear of me going out again, for any reason. He really does make me mad and upset sometimes. He can be right nasty."

Joan didn't stop talking. She told Chrissy that she went to the cave and found the headless horseman's head.

"You know, it wasn't real. It had frightened the life

out of me though. I wonder why somebody is going around acting as though he is the headless horseman."

Chrissy impatiently pushed Joan with her head until Joan finally realized she should take the gag of Chrissy's mouth.

"Thank You, and about time too," said Chrissy who was all flustered. "Untie my hands as well, they are really sore. We will have to wait here a bit in case they come back. We don't want to let them know that we know what they are up to. Then I will tell you the whole story."

Chrissy told Joan everything, about John being the headless horseman and why. About the cottage at the back of the huts and about being in the hut for over twenty-four hours.

"Obviously my dad and John got my note," said Chrissy. "But Joan, you must leave me here and make sure my dad, John and the Police are going to be up at the Wakefield's. Will you ask my dad to come and pick me up before he goes to the hall. I want to see these villains caught and I want to get out of here."

"I am going to see if I can come with you as well," said Joan. "I will think of some excuse to give to my parents and ask your dad if I can go with the two of you. Besides he is going to need help getting you in car."

"See you soon," cried Chrissy. "And hurry because it's getting late."

Joan left the hut and shut the door behind her.

The thought of her being left alone again upset

Chrissy. She tried to reassure herself it wouldn't be for long this time. Then she would be going home after they had caught the thieves, red handed.

CHAPTER THIRTEEN

Caught Red Handed

Night had descended on the hut like a large black cloak encircling everything in site. The night was still, not a sound could be heard, Chrissy felt frightened, terrified. She imagined creatures prowling round the hut. Hungry creatures that thought she would be something tasty to eat. She pushed herself as far back in the corner that she could go. Tears came into her eyes again. She felt so lonely. Minutes seemed like hours and hours seemed like days.

"Please come and get me out of here, Dad," she whispered desperately. "Please come and help me."

Her foot throbbed with pain that had travelled up her leg. It felt like someone had hit her foot with a large mallet. She felt that she couldn't live through this any longer. She felt desolate. Now she could see little men dancing around, they were laughing. Why were they laughing. She was going in out of consciousness, a large foreboding dark figure stood in front of her.

"No, please don't hurt me anymore," she cried. "I hurt so much. Please don't hurt me, please don't touch me. No! No!"

"Chrissy."

Someone was calling her name; someone was shaking her.

"Go away, please don't hurt me anymore," she sobbed uncontrollably.

"Chrissy, its your father," said Sam. "You are getting delirious."

"Dad! Dad! Is that really you. Have you come to save me from the creatures and the little men."

"I think we should take her straight to hospital, Joan."

Chrissy had started to come round. She shouted.

"NO! I want to see those villains caught, then I will go to hospital. Please dad, I have been in this hut nearly two days because of them. I want to see them caught."

"Okay, if you are sure, you can manage it. I have brought you some tablets for pain. Can you get some water out the car please Joan. And here is a chocolate bar, I am sure you could use the energy by eating that."

Sam untied his daughter and slowly rubbed her legs and stretched them out gently. He saw the terrible injury she had to her foot. He strongly felt he should take her straight to the hospital, but he didn't want to upset her anymore.

Joan came into the hut with water and gave it to Chrissy. She drank it thirstily until she had finished the whole bottle.

"Right Chrissy," said Sam. "We are going to help you up. You hold on tightly to Joan and me. Let's get you in the car."

Slowly they managed to get her down the steps of the hut and into the back seat of the car. Someone had kindly put a pillow and some blankets there.

"We will turn left at the top of the hill and take that road to the Hall," said Sam as he drove through the gates out of the quarry yard. "The police think that they will probably take the Lexington Road to the hall. Where they would most likely pull into the courtyard and get in through the kitchen. That's what they did before."

Joan got out of the car and shut the gate behind them. They turned right to go up Pudding Hill and shortly after the top of the hill, turned left on to the Egmund Hall road.

"The police suggested we park near the old stables at the side of the house," said Sam. "They advised the Wakefield's not to turn on the lights outside the stables, that way we can hide in the shadows."

"Where are the Police going to hide," asked Joan.

"They will be all over the place. There will only be one outside light turned on at the Hall tonight, that is where you enter the property on the Lexington entrance. We have been asked to put our lights out when we have site of the hall. And to go very slow."

"At least we won't have to worry about seeing *The Ghost of Pudding Hill,* because he will be at the Hall already." Chrissy feebly laughed.

Joan and Sam felt they should join in. Now they knew who the ghost was it wasn't frightening any more.

"Did John tell Lord Wakefield; he was the ghost yet." Asked Joan.

"I don't think so, he wants to wait until yourself and Chrissy are with him," said Sam. "So, you can help him explain his reasons and about his inheritance."

"Good idea," said Chrissy. "Lord Wakefield has got to understand that John is worthy of Sara. And let them live happily at Fox Hall."

They could now see Egmund Hall come into view. Someone had also left the light on over the main entrance door, which they appreciated. It didn't leave them in complete darkness.

Sam turned his lights off on the car and slowly drove up to the Hall and turned right towards the stables. He parked the car well in the shadows but first he turned the car round to face the front of the Hall so they could see what was going on.

"Now all we can do is wait," said Sam.

Although the evening air was a bit cool, they put the windows down in the car so they could hear what was going on. Whispering to each other in case they missed anything that might be going on. They sat waiting for some time. Again, it seemed like hours to Chrissy.

Suddenly Joan heard another vehicle coming. It sounded like it was coming up through the Lexington entrance. She put her hand to her ear so everyone would listen.

"That must be them," she whispered. "It didn't sound as though they were pulling a trailer or anything though."

"If they had much sense, they would have parked that somewhere and pick it up later," said Sam.

Chrissy and Joan nodded in agreement.

"Now let's wait for some action," whispered Chrissy. "Do you know what the plan of action is Dad?"

"So, they are caught *red handed* the Police hidden inside the hall are going to wait until they actually take their first item, that's when they will take action."

A short time later the lights in Hall went on and there was a lot of noise. Shouting and screaming, running back and forth.

"Yes!" shouted Chrissy. "They have got them."

Dogs were barking, Police were running around. Lady Wakefield came running out of the front door all flustered and in tears, followed by Sara Wakefield who was trying to comfort her mother.

"They have got them now, mother," said Sara. "So don't fret anymore. One of the dogs nipped one of the thieves on the bum, it was so funny."

"Sara," cried Lady Wakefield. "It's not ladylike to say *bum.*"

"My Christine, and Joan have been doing their own investigations into the robberies, at their own risk might I add. They found out who the thieves were and where they had hidden their ill- gotten gains."

"Yes, Lord Wakefield," interrupted Chrissy. "I have been locked in a hut at the old quarry for nearly two days. It was the hut they had everything they had stolen stored in. They had me tied up; and I was injured. I wanted to see them caught and so the Police gave us permission to be here. I really hope you don't mind Sir, but I have been through an awful time."

She showed Lord Wakefield her injured foot.

"Oh, dear me," said Lady Wakefield, as she walked towards the gathering. "That looks dreadful. Bring her into the house. Who was that on horseback and, get down from the roof of that car, Sara. You will get everything dirty."

"It's John Midgley, mother," said Sara proudly. "And he is going to catch that villain."

"Come on in everyone," said Lord Wakefield. "We will get cook to get everyone some refreshments and a nice hot cup of tea. Let me help you with your daughter, Mr. Danvers."

"It's Sam, your lordship, please call me Sam."

The Police had already taken Burt away and had the van driven to the Police Station and impounded. Sergeant Doherty had now joined the party.

"Sergeant Doherty," asked Chrissy. "I know you are not to impressed with me lying to you and I apologise for that, but did you know there is also a small trailer they were towing. That is also full of stolen goods. They must have parked it in a layby or something so they could pick it up later."

"Is that right, miss. I will get a couple of men out there and see if they can locate it."

"I think you might be able to ask, Burt. He is not very smart when Charlie is not around. Especially if you tell him that Charlie has escaped. That will probably really upset him."

"Well, miss, thank you for the information, we will certainly try and get the truth out of Burt. Non of us will know better than you what he is like when he is on a job. After all they had you tied up in that hut for nearly two days, with your foot broken as well."

"Rosaleena," Lady Wakefield turned to her housekeeper who had been bringing in sandwiches and tea. "Can you phone for an ambulance for, Christine. She really must go to hospital to get that foot looked at. It will take them quite a while to get here, they come from Mansfield."

"I understand I should go to the hospital, Lady Wakefield, but I want to see them bring Charlie back."

"I am sure you probably do, Christine. John is a good horseman," said Lord Wakefield. "I am sure he will catch him in no time and like her Ladyship said, it will take the ambulance a while to get here,"

Chrissy nodded her head to acknowledge she understood.

The ambulance arrived an hour later and there was still no sign of John, Charlie and the other Policemen or the Police Dog. Chrissy had to agree to go to the hospital without any argument.

Sam turned round to Joan and asked if she would mind going in the ambulance with Chrissy.

"I will follow in the car, when I have been back to Kirkby to tell your parents briefly what has happened and where you are."

"Yes, thank you Mr. Danvers," said Joan. "They would be furious if they didn't know where I was and turned up in the middle of the night."

Everyone said their good-byes and left the hall. The ambulance went to the hospital in Mansfield, Sam went down to Kirkby to the Parsons and Sergeant Doherty left for the Police Station in Ogmanton.

Before Sergeant Doherty left, he had informed the Wakefield's that he would be back in the morning to make sure everything was alright.

CHAPTER FOURTEEN

Where is Sara Wakefield

Chrissy had broken her foot and twisted her ankle. Joan had been right about that. The Doctors said that if she had come in any later, she likely might have lost her foot. They told her that a break was better than a fracture though because they could pin a break.

Joan had to hold Chrissy's hand tightly when they put her ankle back in place. Poor Chrissy thought she had been in enough pain already, but it was nothing like what she felt at that time.

After fixing the ankle she was told she would have to go into surgery to have the foot bone pinned. By this time Chrissy's father had arrived at the hospital and the doctors took him to one side.

"Excuse me, doctors," shouted Chrissy in a disgruntled voice. "It is my foot, and I would like to hear what you are talking about."

"The doctor said you could be in hospital a few days," said Sam.

"A few days," cried Chrissy. "I have been locked in a hut for nearly two days, I was in old cottage for nearly one and I was stuck in a cave at the quarry nearly all night. I want to go home ASAP. If you don't mind."

"Miss Danvers," said Dr. Bob. "You *will* have to stay in at least two nights, okay! You will have to be put on anti-biotics and an intravenous to build up your strength. I heard you haven't had much to eat for about 3 days."

"Dad," pleaded Chrissy.

"Do what the doctor says, okay. You could still end up losing your foot if you are not careful."

Joan went to Chrissy's side and took her hand.

"I will come with your dad tomorrow night to see you."

"Then if everything is okay," said Sam. "We will bring you home the next day. We will make a bed up for you in the sitting room. Smudge will like that."

"Oh, Smudge. I have missed my Smudge. Give him a hug from me will you, dad."

Dr. Bob gave Chrissy a quizzical look.

"Smudge is my cat, Dr. Bob."

As Chrissy's father and Joan were saying goodbye to Chrissy the nurses came in to get her ready for surgery. Dr. Bob wanted to do the surgery that night and not waste any time.

Chrissy came through the surgery well and without any complications. The surgeons were very pleased. She was sat up in bed anxiously waiting for her breakfast when the doctors came round.

"You are looking quite well, Christine." Said Dr. Bob.

"I am ready for my breakfast," said Christine. "Do you think they might give me two portions."

"You can always ask."

Chrissy had a good breakfast and slept most of the morning. At lunch time she also ate well and was very alert when her father and Joan came in later that afternoon. Joan had managed to get out of school a bit earlier.

The story of Chrissy and Joan's adventures was all round the school and many of the pupils had signed a big card for Chrissy. Joan had a bunch of lovely flowers that she gave to Chrissy.

"My mum sent them for you. They are out of her garden."

Her father gave Chrissy some more cards and some grapes and chocolates. Chrissy felt amazingly spoilt.

"Now for the news," said Sam. "They couldn't find Charlie in the woods and returned to the house about two o'clock this morning. Then everyone went to bed. Unfortunately, Charlie must have returned to the house between two and seven this morning. He kidnapped Sara Wakefield."

Chrissy's mouth hung open in shock.

"Charlie has a way of getting into the house through the kitchen, which was not alarmed again. They have no idea where he has taken her."

"Lord and Lady Wakefield, and John are beside themselves with worry." Said Joan.

"Sergeant Doherty thinks he might hold her for ransom," said Sam. "He wants to get Burt out of Prison and get the van back. They haven't found the trailer yet."

"This is terrible," cried Chrissy. "How frustrating it is being stuck in here as well."

"Christine," shouted Sam. "Don't you get any smart ideas of trying to get out of hospital too soon. You will have too learn to use crutches and they will give you some exercises as well."

"Okay, dad, I won't try anything funny. But I bet Sergeant Doherty is right, I bet he is holding her for ransom. It's just a hunch but if they can find that trailer, it wouldn't surprise me if poor Sara isn't locked in there."

"Maybe its on the Nottingham Road," interrupted Joan. "Remember Charlie and Burt said they were going to Nottingham to see *Micky the Midget.* He buys the stolen goods."

"You must get hold of Sergeant Doherty, dad," said Chrissy. "And tell him what we have just discussed. Thanks for all the goodies you two. I will be alright on my own until I go home tomorrow. Go and see Sergeant Doherty before he goes off shift."

Joan and Sam hugged Chrissy goodbye and left the hospital for Ogmanton Police Station.

The following afternoon Chrissy was given the, *all clear* and was discharged from hospital. She had been given exercises to do and shown how to use the crutches properly. By three pm she was waiting by her bed for her father.

As soon as she was in the car on the way home, she started her questioning.

"Right, dad," asked Chrissy. "What's the news."

Sam told her that they had made it to the Police Station in time before Sergeant Doherty went off shift. They related to him all their ideas and asked if he had any telephone calls from Charlie yet. Apparently, they had that morning. The Sergeant was good enough to let Sam know. They had been right; he was holding Sara Wakefield hostage in exchange for Burt and the Van with the stolen goods in it.

"Have they found the trailer yet, dad."

"They are searching the main Nottingham Road, this afternoon."

"We have to go back through part of *Sherwood Forrest* this afternoon. There are so many pull offs that a trailer could have easily been hidden not far from the road."

"We will try a couple of the obvious ones on the way back," said Sam.

"No, not the obvious ones. Charlie isn't stupid unfortunately, and I don't think it would be too far away from Ogmanton round-a- bout either."

About two miles from the round-a-bout Chrissy's father pulled of the road and searched areas where a trailer could be hidden. Then they realized they should be searching for tire marks. It hadn't rained for a number of days so there should be some tire marks.

About a mile before the round-a-bout they spotted some tire marks that must have been made by a heavy van or lorry. Sam pulled off to the side of the road and got out of the car.

He followed the tracks further into the forest while Chrissy watched intently. He then briefly disappeared behind some trees and returned shortly after with a big smile on his face.

Chrissy felt the excitement overwhelm her; she knew her father had found the trailer. She shouted out the window.

"Dad, knock on the side of the trailer. See if Sara might be locked in there."

He returned to the place he had found the trailer and knocked on the side of it. A faint knock came from within.

"Sara, if that is you, knock twice." Sam shouted.

Just as he had hoped, two knocks came from within the trailer.

"I will be back shortly," shouted Sam. "I have to find something to break the lock."

He rushed back to the car and told Chrissy the news. He went to the boot to find the tire iron, and picked up a blanket in case Sara might be cold and be in her night things.

"Hurry, dad," shouted Chrissy. "She must be terrified."

It wasn't long before he came back from behind the trees with a shivering Sara, wrapped in a blanket. The poor young woman was near to tears.

He helped Sara into the front seat of the car, Chrissy was on the back seat with her leg up. The tears flooded down Sara's face. Chrissy put her arms round her as best she could to comfort her.

"How is Mrs. Midgley," she sniffled.

"What do you mean, how is Mrs. Midgley," asked Sam.

"I think that man must have come in through the kitchen door," said Sara. "I think he knocked her out and shut her in the pantry. I don't think you can open the pantry door from the inside. We went out through the kitchen door."

"That Charlie guy is absolutely ruthless," shouted Chrissy.

"Let's get you home, Sara. You don't mind me calling you Sara, do you."

"Not at all Mr. Danvers."

"I am sure your father won't mind me phoning the Police Station from the Hall. We better tell him where the trailer is and that we have you home. Then we better see if Mrs. Midgley has been found."

Lord and Lady Wakefield were over the moon when Sara went running into the house.

Lady Wakefield called for Rosaleena and asked her to tell Mrs. Midgely to prepare a meal for Sara and then go up and run a bath for her.

"Your, Ladyship," said Rosaleena. "Nobody has seen cook since yesterday. We haven't heard from her, nor has John."

Sara put her hand over her mouth in shock.

"Sam," she cried. "Will you come with me; we think we know where poor Mrs. Midgely is."

Everyone followed Sam and Sara down to the kitchen with Chrissy hopping behind on her crutches. They went straight to the pantry and opened the door.

There was poor Mrs. Midgely on the floor. She had been gagged and tied and was in quite a state, after having spent the night there.

Rosaleena and Sam helped her up and sat her down at the kitchen table. They took the gag of her mouth and untied her hands and feet. She slowly lifted her hand and rubbed her head where Charlie had hit her.

"Oh dear, Mrs. Midgely," soothed Lady Wakefield as she rubbed her hands. "Rosaleena, will you please phone Dr. Duffy and get him to come here as soon as possible.

Briefly explain to him what has happened."

"No, your Ladyship," protested Mrs. Midgely. "I am just a bit bruised, cold and hungry. I am sorry your Ladyship for letting that awful man in the house. I thought it might have been John."

"You weren't to know," said Lord Wakefield. "And look Sara is alright. She is just cold and hungry like you. But Christine and her father found her, we are so pleased to say."

Lady Wakefield shouted to Rosaleena to bring some blankets down when she had finished on the telephone, while they all made their way up to the lounge where a nice warm fire was burning in the grate.

When Rosaleena had finished on the telephone, Sam asked. "May I call Sergeant Doherty and inform him of what is going on and that we found Miss. Wakefield and the trailer with the remainder of the stolen goods."

"I should get Dr. Duffy to look at Sara as well," Lady Wakefield looked concerned and so Lord Wakefield thought it was good idea.

"Now he can examine you one at a time, in my sitting room."

When Rosaleena returned and informed Lady Wakefield that he would be there in about an hour. She handed Sara and Mrs. Midgely a couple of blankets each. Lady Wakefield then asked Rosaleena if she could contact Mrs. Hawthorne at Ponsomby Hall to see if we could borrow their cook for a couple of hours.

"I am sorry to have you running about so much, Rosaleena," said Lady Wakefield. "But it's such an unusual state we are in."

Rosaleena nodded her head.

"I can make you some tea first. Mr. Danvers is on the telephone with the Sergeant Doherty."

When Sam returned to the lounge, he told everyone about the conversation with Sergeant Doherty.

"Chrissy had actually come up with the idea that if they didn't tell Charlie that we had found Miss. Wakefield and the trailer, and then let Charlie have Burt and the van for the return of Miss.Wakefield. In the meantime, the Police would be surrounding the whole area where the trailer is, including towards Mansfield and every exit on the round-a-bout at Ogmanton."

"Apparently Sergeant Doherty had agreed and had mentioned Charlie was supposed to be telephoning him any time soon," said Sam.

"Mrs. Hawthorne's cook should be up here very soon," announced Lady Wakefield and then we will all have a nourishing dinner . In the dining room."

"Oh, your Ladyship," protested Mrs. Midgely. "I couldn't possibly eat in the best dining room."

"Yes, you can, and you shall." Said Lady Wakefield. "You can go up to your room and change your clothes when Dr. Duffy has examined you."

Mrs. Midgely bowed her head in submission.

"Do you mind if we go and get Joan," Chrissy asked. "She has been involved in all of this and would love to know what is going on."

"Of course," said Lord Wakefield. "But Chrissy you stay here, and your father will go. You have had enough excitement, and you have just got out of hospital."

Dr. Duffy arrived and examined both Sara and Mrs. Midgely and gave them the, *all clear*. He had a prescription made out for headache tablets but in the meantime left her a few, so no one had to fill the prescription until tomorrow. He also told them both that they should have an early night and take a sleeping draft each.

"Dr. Duffy, would you stay for dinner," asked Lady Wakefield. "We can then tell you all that has been going on."

Dr. Duffy accepted her Ladyship's invitation and said that he would be honoured. Mrs. Hawthorne's cook, Sadie arrived and started the dinner. While Sara and Mrs. Midgely had a nice warm bath and put on clean clothes. By that time Sam had arrived back with Joan. Dinner was ready to be served.

Sadie had brought her kitchen maid with her and so Lady Wakefield asked Rosaleena to join them. She finally accepted after a great deal of protesting.

The evening meal was delicious, even Mrs. Midgely had to agree. After everyone had retired back to the lounge, Sam and Lord Wakefield had a fine brandy and the ladies had a cup of tea. Then Rosaleena brought Sara's and Mrs. Midgely's sleeping drafts and said her goodnights.

Sadie the cook said she would return later tomorrow after she had got Col. And Mrs. Hawthorne's breakfast and do a breakfast for them.

Everyone said their goodnights and agreed to meet up later the following afternoon and get updates on what was happening.

CHAPTER FIFTEEN

John Got The Seal of Approval

It was a lovely day for good news and that is what everyone was hoping for. Sergeant Doherty had asked everyone concerned to meet up at the Hall. He had Lord and Lady Wakefield's approval and so they decided to open the ballroom and serve tea, beer and wine and sandwiches, small sausage rolls and small cakes. Everyone who had been affected by Charlie and Burt's thieving ways had been invited.

When Chrissy, Joan and Sam arrived there was a few people there already. Sergeant Doherty looked so proud of himself, so they guessed he had caught Charlie and Burt. As soon as he saw them, he came over with a smile on his face as wide as the river Trent.

Taking Chrissy and Joan's hands he announced. "Thanks to you two young ladies and John. Where is John Midgely?"

The Sergeant saw John in background and beckoned him over.

"Thanks to Chrissy and Joan, again, and this time you also John, for helping the Ogmanton Police. We have apprehended the villains Charlie and Burt and retrieved all the stolen goods. Charlie and Burt are now on their way to Nottingham jail and awaiting trial. They will not only be charged for several robberies, but they will also be charged on two counts of kidnapping and causing undue stress, fear and aggravation to yourself, Christine and to Sara Wakefield. And one count of assault and imprisonment to Mrs. Midgely."

Now I am going to inform everyone of what is going on and then my men will help them find their property, which is outside in the van and the trailer.

Sergeant Doherty asked everyone to have a seat as he had an announcement to make. When everyone was seated, and quiet Sergeant Doherty gave his speech. Specifically thanking Christine Danvers, Joan Parsons, John Midgely, who was a true hero riding into the forest to catch Charlie Makepeace. And by no means least Mr. Sam Danvers who did more then his share of running about and helping where he could.

"Would you please stand up, those who I have mentioned," said Sergeant Doherty. "And let us show our appreciation."

A round of applause and three cheers sounded through the ballroom.

"Lady Wakefield has kindly put on refreshments for you all so please help yourselves before you go out to the van and get your property back."

Everyone was milling around and talking and going up to the heroes to shake their hands. Sara made a point of being beside John. Something that Lord and Lady Wakefield quizzically observed.

"They seem to be getting rather close," said Lord Wakefield. "We must ask them about this when everyone has gone."

"Absolutely," replied Lady Wakefield. "Mind you he is a nice enough gentleman and quite well to do after inheriting his uncle's estate. But he is our cook's son."

"Don't worry my dear, we will sort it out."

A couple of hours later the guests started to leave and collect their property. Sergeant Doherty had asked everyone to make a list of everything that been stolen from them so he could hand it to the Solicitors who were taking on the cases. Everyone was very obliging about this.

When nearly everyone had gone Lord Wakefield asked John if he would mind staying behind a while. John had guessed what his Lordship wanted to talk to him about so he asked if Chrissy and Joan could stay behind as well. They had something to say on his behalf.

Lord Wakefield looked a bit put out by this, but he granted John his wishes.

Chrissy's father then came up to the discussion and mentioned that he would have to wait for Chrissy and Joan and that he would also like to say something on John's behalf. Lord Wakefield looked even more confused.

When everyone had gone, including Sergeant Doherty they all went to the lounge. Sara sat on one of the sofas with her mother and listened intently. Of course, she knew what it was all about.

"John, my boy," started Lord Wakefield. "I know you are of great character and an extremely good estate manager and that you have inherited a decent estate of your own. But I have observed that you and Sara seem to be getting rather too friendly. And her Ladyship and I are not sure whether we approve. Your mother is our cook."

"Lord Wakefield, sir," said John. "Sara and I are very much in love."

Sara looked at her farther and mother with pleading eyes.

"We are mother, father. We knew you wouldn't allow us to see each other and so I am sorry, but we have been meeting secretly for quite some time now."

"I am *the present ghost of Pudding Hill,* Sir."

Lady Wakefield jumped back in surprise.

"Sara, what on earth have you been doing."

"Nothing, mother, we just talk and hold hands and walk together near the woods. John dressing up as the ghost was the only way we could think of seeing each other."

"And I thought it was utter twaddle," said Lord Wakefield. "When people had said they had seen the headless horseman again, I thought it was something to do with these thieves."

Chrissy, then interrupted.

"Forgive me for interrupting, your Lordship, your Ladyship. But if it hadn't have been for John I could have suffered from exhaustion as well hunger and my injuries. He put me on his horses back and took me to the old cottage that used to belong to his uncle. He knew I was in danger. He is such a kind, caring and sensible gentleman."

"And your Ladyship, your Lordship," interrupted Joan. "Times are changing, and new money is coming in and buying big houses and estates. You know John; that makes a big difference to someone else coming along and wanting to marry Sara your Lordship, your ladyship. John's estate has over four hundred acres of good arable and grazing land. And the house is quite large."

"I know it's a bit of an embarrassment John's mother being your cook," said Chrissy. "But I have an idea; I am sure Sara doesn't know how to run a household properly. Maybe Mrs. Midgely can be their housekeeper, as well as Sara's mother-in-law. There is nothing demeaning about that. Is there."

"You probably didn't know this, your Lordship, your Ladyship," interrupted Joan. "But Mrs. Midgely was quite upset when you brought Rosaleena back with you when you returned from your holidays. She says she knows the house back to front as she has been with you quite a long time."

"Oh dear," said Lady Wakefield. "I didn't know that Mrs. Midgely might want to be the housekeeper when the old housekeeper left."

"You know my mother is not one to interrupt or get in the way," said John. "She is a very smart lady, but she says she knows her place if that is her lot in life. She would be overjoyed to be our housekeeper, if that would suit Sara, that is. And have you seen her dressed up; she can be as smart as any Lady."

"What is your mother's first name, John," asked Lord Wakefield.

"It's Rosemary, your Lordship, a very pretty name I think."

Everyone agreed.

"You are right, Joan," said Lady Wakefield. "People from middle class backgrounds are coming into money. Your uncle made his money in Australia, didn't he John."

"Yes, your Ladyship, a very smart man and sensible. Although the Midgely Ladies in the family were all cooks. You have to remember my mother is not a true Midgely, she only married into the family."

"I know this is a family affair," said Lord Wakefield. "But you have all been good to my family and are friends of John So, her Ladyship and I will think deeply on this matter, and we will make our decision by Saturday. Don't you agree my dear."

"Yes, I do agree. And I would like you all to come to afternoon tea at four o'clock. I have enjoyed entertaining these few days."

At four o'clock Saturday afternoon everyone was congregated in Egmund Hall's large lounge again but this time they had on their Sunday best. Chrissy and Joan were dressed in pretty blue dresses. Sara was wearing a smart fashionable yellow shift dress with stiletto healed shoes. She only wore a little makeup, she looked beautiful. Mrs. Midgely was there in a smart pale green suit and of course her ladyship was impeccably dressed in a cream two piece.

All the men had shirts and ties on. John and Sam wore sports jackets and his Lordship a suit.

Sara and John could not take their eyes off each other.

"The hired help is going to bring in sandwiches and dainty cakes and tea in a minute, but first we will not keep you in suspense any longer. We have made a decision, which Lord Wakefield will announce now."

"Yes," said Lord Wakefield. "After a great deal of thought we decided that John and Sara would be well suited and they seem to be very much in love, which is very important to her Ladyship and I as we married for love also."

Meanwhile Rosaleena had come into the room and was pouring out champagne, which she handed round to everyone, including Chrissy and Joan.

Lord Wakefield gave Sara and John his blessing and everyone raised their glasses to drink their health.

"To Sara and John."

"Now, young man," said Lord Wakefield. "You better take care of my daughter."

"Absolutely, your Lordship, there will be no question of that."

"Also, John, I would still like you to manage this estate, and make sure there are no more ghosts coming up to the property."

Everyone laughed heartily.

Sara asked Chrissy and Joan to be two of her bridesmaids. She said she would have quite a few. But she would like them to be two of them. The girls were honoured.

"You should be alright by then, Christine," said Lady Wakefield. "I would like to request, Sara and John that you won't get married for a year. That is not too long of an engagement."

"Talking about engagement," John interrupted. "I have brought a ring in hope that you would consent to us getting married and that I get *your seal of approval.*"

John pulled from his pocket a beautiful ring box and opened it to reveal an exquisite Diamond Solitaire ring. He got down on one knee and asked Sara to marry him. Of course, she excepted, and the ring slipped on her finger like a glove.

Milton Keynes UK
Ingram Content Group UK Ltd.
UKHW010618291123
433416UK00001B/34

9 798889 635109